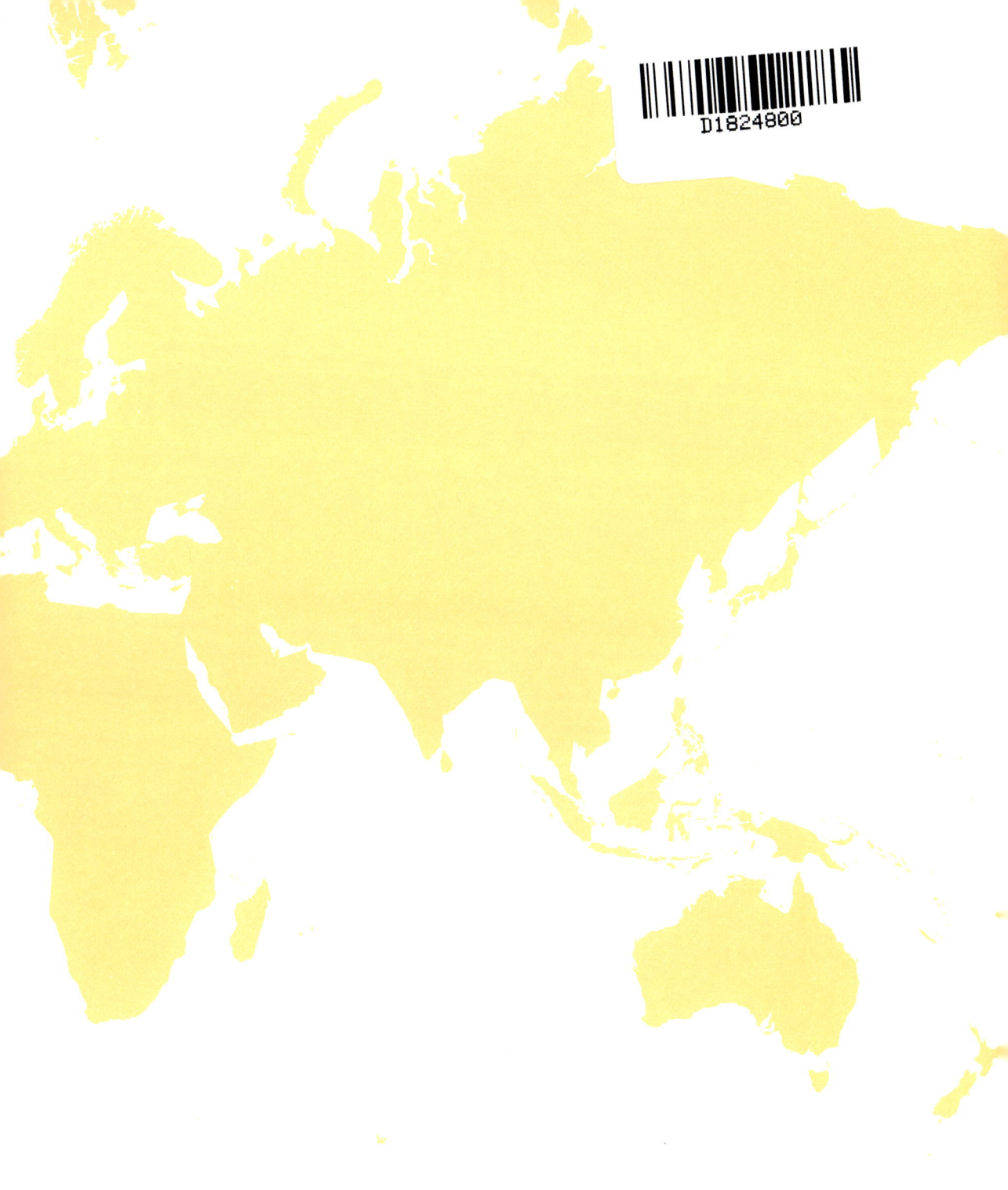

border to border · teen to teen · border to border · teen to teen · border to border

TEENS IN MOROCCO

Global connections

Teens in Morocco

Morocco

by Sandy Donovan

Content Adviser: Susan Schaefer Davis, Ph.D.,
Independent Scholar and Consultant,
Haverford, Pennsylvania

Reading Adviser: Alexa L. Sandmann, Ed.D.,
Professor of Literacy,
Kent State University

Compass Point Books Minneapolis, Minnesota

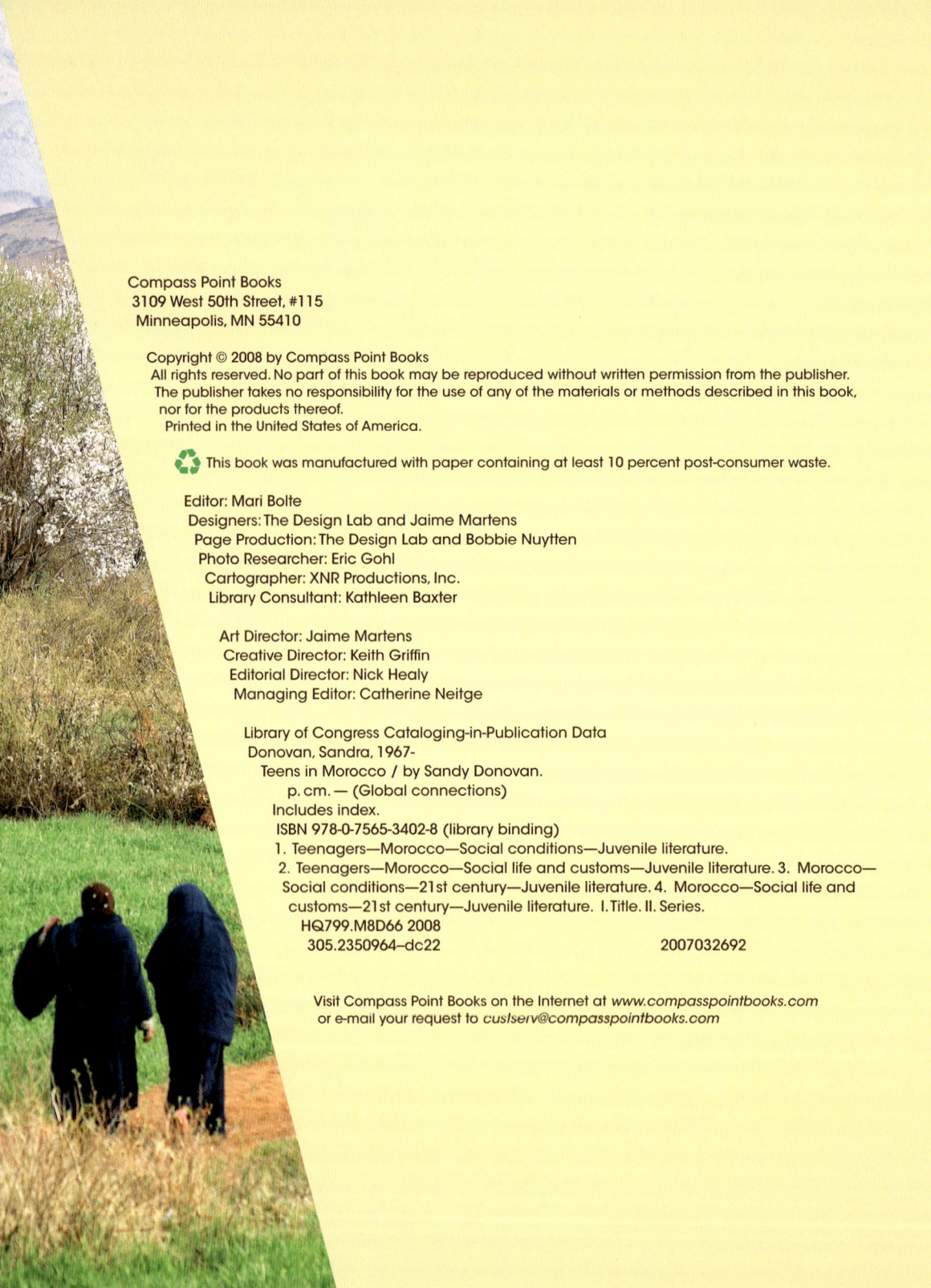

Compass Point Books
3109 West 50th Street, #115
Minneapolis, MN 55410

♻ This book was manufactured with paper containing at least 10 percent post-consumer waste.

Editor: Mari Bolte
Designers: The Design Lab and Jaime Martens
Page Production: The Design Lab and Bobbie Nuytten
Photo Researcher: Eric Gohl
Cartographer: XNR Productions, Inc.
Library Consultant: Kathleen Baxter

Art Director: Jaime Martens
Creative Director: Keith Griffin
Editorial Director: Nick Healy
Managing Editor: Catherine Neitge

Library of Congress Cataloging-in-Publication Data
Donovan, Sandra, 1967-
    Teens in Morocco / by Sandy Donovan.
        p. cm. — (Global connections)
    Includes index.
    ISBN 978-0-7565-3402-8 (library binding)
    1. Teenagers—Morocco—Social conditions—Juvenile literature.
    2. Teenagers—Morocco—Social life and customs—Juvenile literature. 3. Morocco—
    Social conditions—21st century—Juvenile literature. 4. Morocco—Social life and
    customs—21st century—Juvenile literature. I. Title. II. Series.
    HQ799.M8D66 2008
    305.2350964–dc22   2007032692

Visit Compass Point Books on the Internet at www.compasspointbooks.com
or e-mail your request to custserv@compasspointbooks.com

Table of Contents

ATLANTIC
OCEAN

CANADA

U.S.A.

NORWAY

SCOTLAND
NORTHERN
IRELAND UNITED
KINGDOM DENMARK

IRELAND ENGLAND
WALES NETH.
BELGIUM GERMANY
LUX.

FRANCE SWITZERLAND

ANDORRA ITALY

PORTUGAL
SPAIN

TUNISIA M

MOROCCO

Canary Islands

ALGERIA

WESTERN SAHARA

MAURITANIA

⊛
Rabat

SENEGAL

GAMBIA

GUINEA BISSAU

GUINEA

SIERRA LEONE

BENIN
TOGO

NIGERIA

CAMEROON

EQUATORIAL GUINEA

SAO TOME & PRINCIPE

GABON

BRAZIL

ATLANTIC
OCEAN

FINLAND
ESTONIA
LATVIA
LITHUANIA
POLAND
BELARUS
SLOVAKIA
HUNGARY
OATIA
ROMANIA
OSNIA
YUGOSLAVIA
MACEDONIA
BULGARIA
ALBANIA
GREECE
UKRAINE
MOLDOVA
RUSSIA

MONGOLIA
KAZAKHSTAN
KYRGYZSTAN
UZBEKISTAN
TAJIKISTAN
CH

TURKEY
GEORGIA
AZERBAIJAN
ARMENIA
TURKMENISTAN
AFGHANI

CYPRUS
LEBANON
ISRAEL
SYRIA
IRAQ
IRAN
ESH

JORDAN
KUWAIT
OMAN
QATAR
U.A.E
OMAN

LIBYA
EGYPT
SAUDI ARABIA

CHAD
SUDAN
YEMEN
ERITREA
DJIBOUTI
SOMALIA

INDIAN OCEAN

SRI LANKA

CENTRAL AFRICAN REPUBLIC

GO
DEMOCRATIC REPUBLIC
OF THE CONGO
RWANDA
BURUND
TANZANIA

ANGOLA
MALAWI
MOZAMBIQUE

TEENS IN MOROCCO

TEENS IN MOROCCO LIVE IN A MELTING POT OF CULTURES.
While their country is young—Morocco has only been an independent nation since 1956—their culture is thousands of years old. It has influences from Roman, Arab, French, and Spanish settlers, as well as the indigenous Berbers, or Amazigh people.

While Morocco is located on the African continent, most of its customs and culture come from either Arab and Berber Muslims, who ruled the area for centuries, or the French, who governed the region for the first half of the 20th century.

One might meet urban Moroccan teens who speak French, dress like Europeans, and ride a moped—although most speak Arabic and walk. Rural teens may speak a Berber dialect, wear a traditional long robe, and ride a donkey. Whatever their lifestyle, Moroccan teens are well aware that they are the future of their country   nearly half of all Moroccans are under the age of 20.

Although girls are less likely to attend school than boys, the enrollment rate for both sexes is steadily increasing.

1

Learning at School

TWO DOZEN MOROCCAN 13-YEAR-OLDS LISTEN INTENTLY AS THEIR TEACHER GOES OVER MATH PROBLEMS ON A BLACKBOARD. The students sit at scratched wooden desks neatly lined up in a small classroom. The desks are quite old, but the classroom is brand new. Still, it is far from modern. It has a concrete floor and plywood walls with four small windows that let in the sunlight. Inside the room, it's hot and stuffy, but the students are lucky to have their own classroom and teacher. Morocco's fast-growing young population makes it hard for the govern-

ment to build schools and hire enough teachers to educate everyone.

Although everyone ages 6 to 15 is required to go to school in Morocco, only about half attend. More boys attend school than girls, and younger children are more likely to be in school than older students. In 2004, 89 percent of males and 84 percent of females of primary-school age were enrolled. These numbers drop by at least half by the time they reach high school age.

The percentage of children in school varies widely throughout the country. In the densely populated, major cities of Casablanca, Agadir, Rabat, and Fes, about 80 percent of all school-age children are in school. What keeps the other 20 percent out of school is often a lack of money to buy clothing and books, or the need to work to help the family. In the country's more remote areas—including the central lowlands and plains, as well as the Rif and Atlas mountain ranges—school attendance is usually lower. What keeps many children out of school is often a lack of buildings and teachers. In the small villages of these areas, children often must stay home to work with their parents and help provide for their families. Many schools are too far away for the youngest children to walk to them. Other children choose not to attend, and instead begin working. They may think the benefits of employment are greater than the benefits of education.

Inside the Classroom: Basic Education

After six years of primary school, students move on to three years of middle school, called college in

Low Literacy

Morocco's literacy rate is among the lowest in sub-Saharan Africa. In 2004, it was just 52 percent. This means that only 52 of every 100 adults are able to read. Women have a much lower rate than men. The government is working toward increasing both school attendance and literacy; in fact, it spends more than one-fourth of its budget on education. This emphasis seems to be making a difference. While 52 percent is quite low, it is a positive change from 45 percent, which was the rate 10 years ago. Even more promising, the rate for young people is much higher—nearly 81 percent of males and 60 percent of females ages 15 to 24 can read.

Morocco. (The term university is used for higher education.) Together, these first nine years of school are called Basic Education.

Like many aspects of life in Morocco, education incorporates both French and Arabic traditions. In their first years of primary school, Moroccan children study one of two education tracks. The "traditional" track is available for young children who want to learn about Islam, Morocco's official religion. Lessons concentrate on the Qur'an, or the holy book of Islam.

Although female school attendance and literacy have been lower than those of boys, Morocco has made a special effort since the late 1990s to encourage girls to attend school.

Teen Scenes

In Casablanca, Morocco's biggest city, a 13-year-old girl finishes breakfast with her family and grabs her book bag. She has a 10-minute walk to her college, or middle school, and she'll stop to pick up a few friends along the way. She likes to get to school early enough to go over her lessons and homework from the day before. Even though she is only in her first year of middle school, she is already thinking about exams two years away. She hopes to go on to a university and become a doctor. She knows that she needs to be at the top of her class to realize that dream.

Meanwhile, another 13-year-old Moroccan girl is also finishing breakfast. Instead of heading off to school, though, she will help her mother and then join the rest of her family in the fields. She lives on her family's small farm, and everyone is expected to help out during harvest season. Her older brother is planning to move to the city after the harvest to look for work, but she will stay to help her mother take care of her younger sisters and her elderly grandparents.

In Rabat, another young teen gets ready for the day. She attends a private, co-ed school run by an American committee. There are never any shortages of teachers or equipment, and the class sizes are small. The school is expensive, but her family feels it is important for her to get the best education possible. She plans to move to Europe or the United States after finishing school.

The lives of these three young Moroccans are vastly different, but they all reflect certain values. Moroccan families are close, and young people work hard—whether at schoolwork, farm work, or other work—to contribute to their families and improve their own lives.

Memorization of the Qur'an is a common form of learning in Islamic schools.

Older children can take these classes after regular school.

The "modern" track, which most Moroccan students follow, is based on the French school system. The French system was introduced to Morocco during the more than 40 years that most of Morocco was a French protectorate (1912-1956). This track is still taught in Arabic, Morocco's official language, but it emphasizes European history and philosophies. A third, "technical," track is available for students who have finished basic education. This track develops job-related skills. All students, regardless of their chosen track, also begin studying French in their third year, about age 9.

From October through June, young

Moroccans attend primary school for 28 hours a week. During a typical day, students read and write Arabic for two hours (and French for an hour or two, for those age 9 and older). They also have an hour of Islamic studies and an hour of math. Once a week, students have science, art, and physical education. Each day at lunchtime, children head home to share a meal with their families. As they return for their afternoon lessons, the streets near schools come alive with shouts in both French and Arabic.

Moroccan students take their studying seriously. They receive grades in every subject and have to "pass" into each new grade. Students get particularly nervous because they also have to pass a standard exam in the sixth grade, called the *shHada,* to move into middle school for seventh, eighth, and ninth grade. Those who pass this exam are proud of themselves, but they now have to add more than an hour of school each day. The number of hours of school jumps from 28 per week in primary school to 33 to 35 per week in ninth grade. In middle school, students focus less on reading and writing

shHada
shuh-HADA

French Influence

If it seems as if Moroccans use a lot of French words, it's because they do! During the 44 years that France controlled Morocco, the French built schools based on their system. After Morocco gained its independence, the government began revamping the education system, putting more emphasis on the Arabic language and the study of Islamic religion and culture. But much of the French system remained, and the language is still widely used.

Morocco
Topographical
map

SPAIN

Mediterranean Sea

Tangier •

Ceuta (SPAIN)

Melilla (SPAIN)

Er Rif Mts.

Rabat ☆

Sebou River

Casablanca •

Taza Depression

Middle Atlas Mts.

ATLAS MOUNTAINS

Marrakech •

High Atlas Mts.

Anti-Atlas Mts.

ALGERIA

ATLANTIC OCEAN

N
W · E
S

Drâa River

Laâyoune •

Saquia el Hamra

0   100   200 mi.
0   100   200 km

Western Sahara (administered by MOROCCO)

Dakhla •

MAURITANIA

and more on social studies and physical and natural sciences.

At the end of ninth grade, students face not just one standardized exam but two: a schoolwide exam and a country-wide exam. Much of the year is spent preparing for these exams. Together, the tests determine whether students go on to more school, and, if they do go on, which school they will go to. About half of all ninth-graders end their education after middle school. They receive a Certificat d'Etudes Secondaires, or Secondary-School Certificate, and look for work or begin a job.

Moving on to Secondary School

Nearly 2 million Moroccans enroll in secondary school each year. High school attendance is higher for boys than for girls. While nearly 45 percent of boys across Morocco attend high school, only about 35 percent of girls do.

Most students who receive the highest scores on their ninth-grade exams are offered a place in a "general track" at a secondary school. These students prepare for a university and choose among language arts, experimental sciences, and math. Other students who do well on the ninth-grade

A Country of Linguists

French, the unofficial second language of Morocco, is taught as early as the third grade. The language of Morocco's former colonizer is widely used in government and business. Students who live in Morocco's rural areas often speak Amazigh at home. English is becoming more and more common in business and tourism. Since 2002, all Moroccan schools have been required to offer English. Another popular language—especially along Morocco's northern coast—is Spanish. Spain controlled the northern part of Morocco for many years and continues to influence the northern regions of the country.

By the end of secondary school, more than three-quarters of the students enrolled are boys.

exam can enter the "professional" or "technical" tracks at a secondary school. They may concentrate in engineering, economics, or agriculture.

These students may go on to a university or look for a job after high school.

For the first year of high school, students in the general and technical tracks take the same courses. It is during this "common" year that they choose their concentration for the following two years. Depending on the track and concentration, they will spend between 27 and 36 hours per week in the classroom. An additional 20 or more hours may be spent on homework.

In June, students take university-entrance tests. These tests are known as

Middle School Subjects

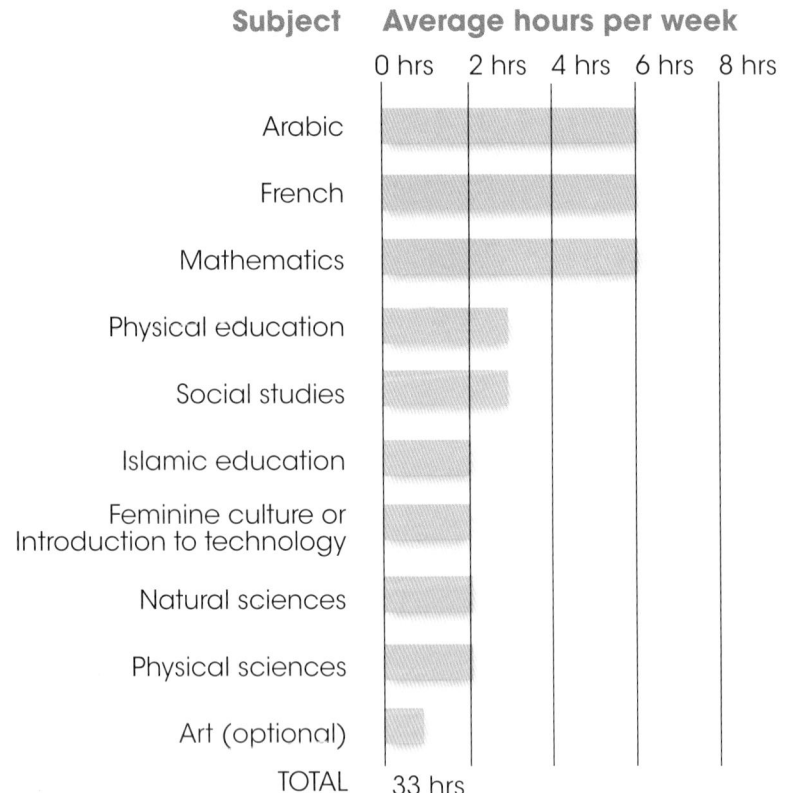

Subject	Average hours per week
Arabic	
French	
Mathematics	
Physical education	
Social studies	
Islamic education	
Feminine culture or Introduction to technology	
Natural sciences	
Physical sciences	
Art (optional)	
TOTAL	33 hrs

After visiting Moroccan schools, Queen Rania of Jordan said: In many ways, education is a "social vaccine" for girls ... it immunizes against untimely death, poverty, and unemployment, and helps them build healthy, hopeful futures.

baccalauréat exams. To graduate and receive a baccalauréat degree, students must take two exams: a regional exam in their first year that covers basic subjects, and, in their second year, a nationwide final exam that accounts for half of their overall score. In some subjects, students are graded entirely on course-work and test scores throughout the year.

baccalauréat
bahk-ah-low-ree-at

These tests are not easy to pass—in 2007, the pass rate was less than 40 percent. Students blame the low rate on difficult tests, insufficient time allowed, the quality of their education, and the country's low literacy rate. However, some teachers cite the students' lack of ability. One teacher said:

If the pass rates are still low, it's because they reflect the true abilities of candidates. The exams are there to ensure that the better students get through.

The education ministry feels that the tests should measure the students' entire education. To the ministry, the low scores show failures of the students and the school system. Recently the government has made changes to improve test scores. Decreasing the number of tests from as many as seven to three or four was a popular decision. Efforts to stop cheating, mainly by

World's Oldest University

Morocco's University of Al Karaouine, in the ancient city of Fes, is considered the oldest university in the world. The school was founded more than 1,000 years ago. (Shishi Middle School in China, formed in 143 B.C., is the oldest educational institution, but not the oldest university.) There are another 12 public (state-funded) universities and one private nonprofit university in Morocco, Al-Akhawayn, which is an English-language, American-style school that awards master's degrees. Altogether, there are about 230,000 university students. Other students who have received a technical baccalauréat degree can enter a two-year technical university program and receive a Brevet de Technicien Supérieur degree.

University education is highly valued in Morocco, and it is seen as a way for individuals to raise both their social status and their standard of living.

forbidding the use of mobile phones during the test, were less popular.

In the past, students with low scores on the first test were allowed to enter the second year anyway. Today students and their families decide whether they should continue or repeat the year and try to do better. Committees approve or deny the decisions.

European trends and fashions impact the way Moroccan teens think, dress, and behave.

2 Daily Life

ONCE SCHOOL IS OUT FOR THE DAY—USUALLY BY MIDAFTERNOON—MOST MOROCCAN STUDENTS HEAD HOME TO HELP WITH CHORES OR BEGIN HOME-WORK. The journey home may take an hour or more, and not because they live far from school. Moroccans have a relaxed view about time in general and tend not to rush from place to place. Visiting with friends, greeting neighbors, and admiring the scenery is an important part of any travel in this country. Like many Muslims, most Moroccans feel that things usually happen when God wills them to. One of the most common phrases in Morocco and other Muslim countries is "Insha'Allah", or "God Willing."

Insha' Allah
in-SHA-allah

City Life

Sunlight trickles down through the trellises hanging high above a maze of narrow, winding streets. The sparkling light only adds to the bustling atmosphere of cobblestone lanes jammed with people of all ages, rickety carts, bicycles, and the occasional moped whizzing by. This is the

Some medina streets are only 2 feet (60 centimeters) wide. Others open onto neighborhood squares.

medina, the ancient walled city—built by Arab settlers as early as the 1200s—that is the heart of every modern Moroccan city. Small openings lead from the bustling streets into shops crowded with displays of crafts like embroidered clothing, hand-woven rugs, carved wooden furniture, and delicate jewelry. In nearby workshops, craftspeople are hard at work. This is where Moroccans come to shop. After school, the already busy streets fill with teens coming to visit friends or getting ready to work. Some families—often the poorest ones—live in small houses on the medina's winding streets.

While Morocco has historically been a rural country, cities are becoming more and more crowded. Young adults flock there in search of work. Today an estimated 55 percent of Moroccans live in cities and towns. Almost all large towns and cities have two distinct areas: the mazelike, medieval medina and the surrounding "new towns." These new towns—as most Moroccans still call them—were first built by the French early in the 20th century to house government buildings, hospitals, and schools. They also included European–style houses for French business owners and government leaders.

Today wealthier Moroccans may live in these areas, which have green

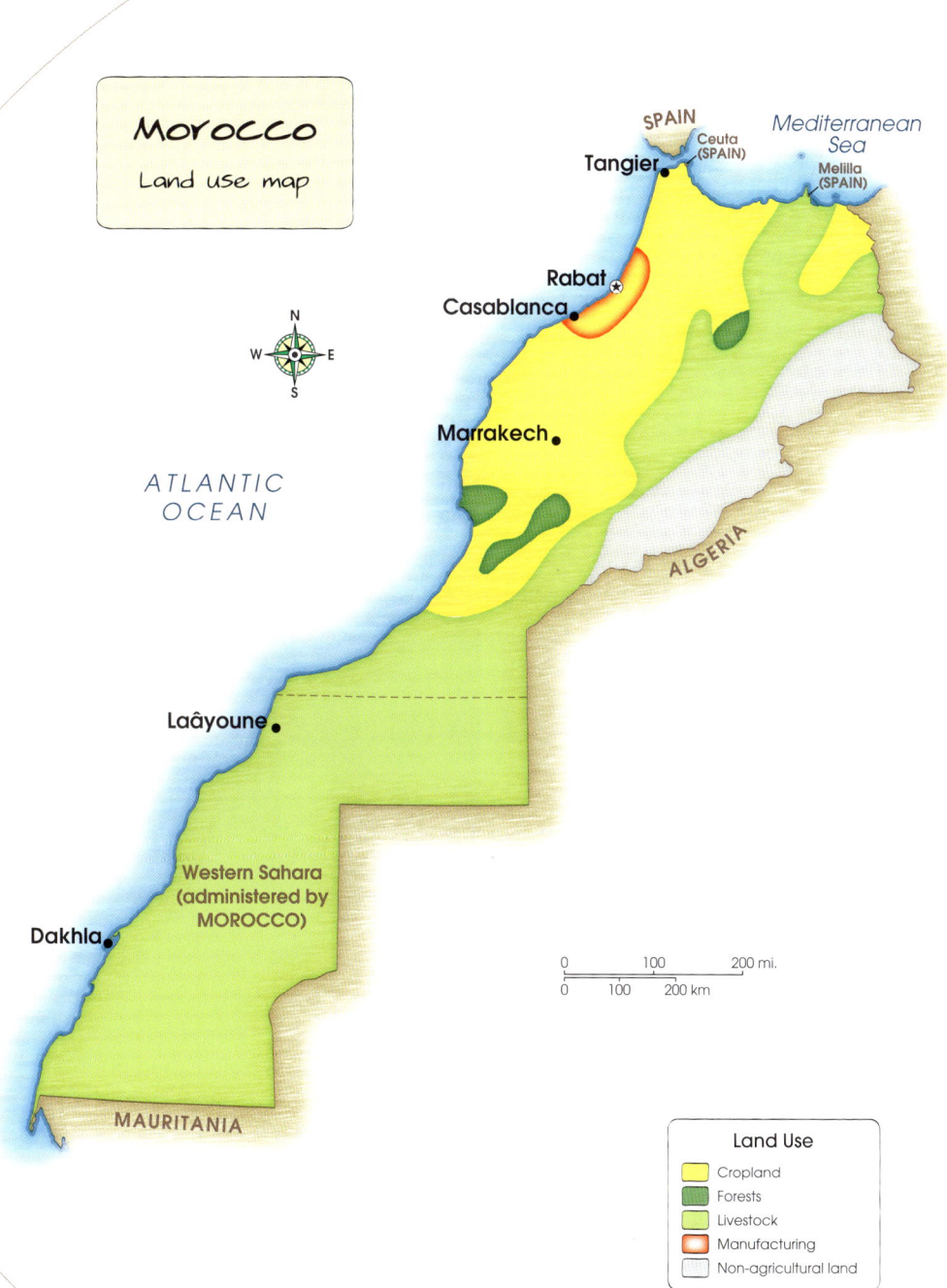

Morocco

Land use map

SPAIN

Mediterranean Sea

Ceuta (SPAIN)

Melilla (SPAIN)

Tangier

Rabat

Casablanca

Marrakech

ATLANTIC OCEAN

ALGERIA

N
W   E
S

Laâyoune

Western Sahara (administered by MOROCCO)

Dakhla

MAURITANIA

0   100   200 mi.
0   100   200 km

Land Use

- Cropland
- Forests
- Livestock
- Manufacturing
- Non-agricultural land

lawns and landscaped flower gardens along broad avenues. The very wealthy live in large, modern houses in parts of the city often called "California"—so called because the neighborhoods resemble those in the U.S. state. Since the 1980s suburbs housing various social classes have been built around Moroccan cities.

In both the medinas and new towns, population growth has led to crowding. Even the paved avenues of the new towns are jammed with buses, taxis, cars, and mopeds. Most teens walk, bike, or take public buses to get where they are going, but some wealthier teens own mopeds. Even when they turn 18, the legal age for driving, many continue to drive mopeds rather than cars. The motorized scooters, which are much easier to navigate, outnumber cars by about 500 to 1.

As more and more Moroccans move into the cities to find work, run-down shantytowns, known as *bidonvilles*, are growing on the edges of many cities. Poor families live in these makeshift housing areas often without running water or electricity.

Morocco's slum dwellers have become targets for religious fundamentalists. In recent years, the majority of Morocco's suicide bombers have been

bidonvilles
bee-DOHN-veels

from the country's shantytowns. It is believed that mistrust of politicians, poor treatment from police, and poor living conditions have encouraged some residents to side with political terrorists. However, an analyst on the Middle East has a different idea:

... [S]hantytowns provide a safe haven for criminals and terrorists. Police

Morocco's King Mohammed VI has publicly stated that poverty is the country's most serious social issue. The country has planned to spend 5.5 billion dirhams (U.S.$701 million) between 2004 and 2010 on a program aimed at eradicating Morocco's shantytowns.

avoid the shantytowns because they get lost in their tight alleys. Mailmen, tax collectors, and water companies steer clear of them too. The state's presence is minimal to nonexistent.

To counter the problems, King Mohammed VI has made it his goal to rid Morocco of its shantytowns by 2010.

The health of Moroccan teens depends on several things. City teens who go to school and live with working parents tend to have access to health care. However, many of the poorest children—whose parents live in the most crowded areas of the bidonvilles—may not even have direct access to clean drinking water or toilets. The World Health Organization states that

100 percent of urban Moroccans have access to health care, but in rural areas it is only available to 65 percent. About 39 of every 1,000 Moroccan children die in their first year of life.

Country Life

Inside her family's house in a small northern village, a 15-year-old girl lights a fire in an oven. She rose before sunrise to help prepare breakfast for her family, which includes two older brothers, a younger sister, her parents,

and her grandparents. In the dark, she mixes lentils and chickpeas for soup, a traditional Moroccan breakfast. Her father and brothers will need to eat a full meal before heading out to work. The girl will stay home to help her mother care for her grandparents. Both of them are ill and elderly, but retirement homes are almost unheard of in Morocco. The girl and her mother try to keep them comfortable, feeding and bathing them each day.

Teens living in rural Morocco—

Transportation options in Morocco include buses, bicycles, camels, horses, cars, and good old-fashioned walking.

In some parts of Morocco, donkeys and bicycles are the only way to get around.

In some desert areas of southern Morocco, groups of extended families still follow a seminomadic lifestyle that has been around for centuries. These clans travel with flocks of sheep and herds of goats during part of the year, seeking places with enough water for themselves and their livestock. In the colder winter months, they will return to their permanent homes.

The appeal of cities, which offer both jobs and excitement, has drawn young people, especially men, away from rural Morocco. The International Fund for Agricultural Development says:

The typical migrant is a young man or woman pushed by both poverty and social pressures to migrate, and drawn by the attractions of a better life. For young men, migration is a door to independence and maturity.

This means that many small villages and towns are now mostly female. Many rural families make a living from farming. During peak seasons, teens find attending school difficult. Some rural communities have changed their school year to fit the late fall and early summer planting and harvesting. Whether they have attended school or not, rural teens usually head for the city to look for work by age 15 or 16. It's common for one sibling—almost always a girl—to stay behind and take care of parents and grandparents.

Health care in rural areas is much harder to find than in cities. Less than 20 percent of Moroccans in the most remote areas have access to health care. This is because of the harsh terrain and the long distances between houses and hospitals. The lack of access to doctors or other trained health professionals makes childbirth particularly risky. In some parts of rural Morocco, more than 100 of every 1,000 babies die within the first year of life, which is quite high, especially when compared with the rest of Northern Africa.

Oranges are a common Moroccan crop, and orange juice is a popular beverage. A glass usually costs between 3 and 4 dirhams (U.S. 38-51 cents).

Favorite Foods

It's noon on Friday, and a 14-year-old girl sits with her family around a table. In the center is a large bowl of grains of semolina pasta covered with a fragrant sauce and carrots, cabbage, squash, and other vegetables. In the center of the dish is a piece of lamb. This is *couscous*, Morocco's national dish, and this family, like many in Morocco, commonly eats it every Friday. The women reach with their right hand—using the left would be rude—and grab a small mound of the pasta. Then, by lightly squeezing and tossing it, they form it into a ball and pop it into their mouths.

couscous
koos-koos

The slowly steamed pasta is served with the stewed meat and vegetables. There are many varieties of couscous—sometimes it is served with chickpeas, and other times raisins or dates are added. Some families serve couscous highly spiced with red pepper.

Gathering with family members for meals is a favorite activity, and food is an important part of the country's culture. In his Moroccan cookbook, author Hassan M'Souli writes, "The art of hospitality is legendary in Morocco, and eating is very much a social ritual, as well as a necessity." Both rural and urban Moroccans continue to enjoy the same traditional dishes—although country residents are more likely to sit on cushions and use their hands or bread instead of silverware. City dwellers are more likely to use Western-style chairs and serving spoons during meals.

Morocco provides a natural supply of excellent ingredients. Fruits

Souks

Inside every large city's medina and small town's square is a spot reserved for a *souk*, or daily food marketplace. In the past, people could only buy fresh meat and vegetables once a week, but now nearly everyone can shop daily. Permanent stalls are set up where vendors sell fruit, vegetables, meats, spices, and other food items. Other items for sale include carpets, jewelry, and crafts. Food vendors arrive before dawn to set up their displays, and for more than 12 hours the souk is jammed with shoppers bargaining. There are also weekly souks in many parts of the country.

souk
sook

A colorful dish called tajine is a traditional Moroccan meat and vegetable stew.

and vegetables like oranges, lemons, tomatoes, olives, and figs grow in many areas of the country. Colorful, fragrant spices like saffron and cumin are easy to find; seafood is abundant along the coasts. Sheep, poultry, and goats thrive throughout the region.

One of Morocco's most common meals is a *tajine*, or stew. Lamb or chicken is sautéed with spices, includ-

ing saffron, cumin, coriander, and crushed red pepper. It is then stewed with olives, garlic, and onion, or perhaps peas and artichoke hearts. The meat is traditionally simmered in this mixture for several hours in a special tajine pot. These earthenware

tajine
tah-jeen

dishes include a flat platter with a ridge and a fitted lid shaped like a cone.

Once the meat in the pot is fall-apart tender, the meal can begin. Seated on cushions around a low, round table, the diners pull off warm pieces of Morocco's famous round bread to scoop up the meat and sop up the sauce. This bread is a staple at almost every meal—in poorer households it may be an entire meal. Bread in Morocco is considered so sacred that if a piece falls on the floor, a diner will pick it up and kiss it. Leftover bread is tradition-ally never thrown away—many families collect their leftover bread and donate it to the poor.

Special events such as births and marriages are marked by celebratory meals. Highlighting the first course at one of these banquets is often a *b'stilla*, an intricate dish of overlapping pastry surrounding a creamy center of meat and eggs. In much of Morocco, the pre-

There are many regional versions of b'stilla. The classic recipe is said to have originated in Fes.

ferred filling for a b'stilla is pigeon meat, but in some areas chicken or seafood is used instead. Sometimes an almond milk and rice b'stilla is served as dessert instead of as a first course. A *mechoui*, or barbecue, is commonly the centerpiece of a banquet. An entire lamb is rubbed with garlic and spices and roasted whole in a heated pit. Afterward, guests use bread or simply their right hands to pull tender meat from the cooked lamb. For dessert, a special dish such as a sweet b'stilla, a rice pudding flavored with raisins and orange-flower water, or a sweet couscous is served. An elegantly arranged platter of fresh fruit ends the meal.

b'stilla
be-STEE-ah
mechoui
MESH-wee

By far the most popular Moroccan drink is a very sweet, mint-flavored green tea. Both young and old people enjoy it at meals, in the morning, and during breaks throughout the day. Yogurt drinks and fruit juices—such as orange, grape, and pomegranate—are also common. Teens often buy fruit-flavored sodas, while adults may enjoy spiced coffee or coffee with milk. Since almost all Moroccans are Muslim, and drinking alcohol goes against their beliefs, wine and beer are never served, and are only available for sale from special stores and at certain times.

Sweet Treats

Moroccans eat sweet b'stillas or couscous at celebratory banquets, but they can also enjoy sweet cakes and pastries any day of the week. Pastry shops, featuring small cakes and finely layered pastries, are often the busiest areas of a market. Moroccan teens may buy fresh doughnuts strung on a loop of reeds or grasses, and women purchase assortments of pastries to serve to friends and family. The pastries come in various shapes: round, triangular, or long and thin like a cigar. Cakes are flavored with ground almonds, cinnamon, water distilled from orange blossoms, or rose petals. Pastries are filled with minced fruit like dates or raisins and then dipped in honey or sprinkled with sugar.

whether along the Mediterranean or Atlantic coasts, or in the central plains, the southern desert, or the Rif or Atlas mountain ranges—lead a much different life than their urban peers. Not only are they less likely to go to school, but they also are more likely to have fewer modern conveniences, like running water or electricity. While some city teens zoom around on mopeds, country teens are more likely to ride donkeys. Some rural families might own a sturdy vehicle, like a pickup truck, that can navigate the rough roads—but they are unlikely to own one of the French cars that are popular in cities.

Housing styles vary throughout the Moroccan countryside. Traditional, courtyard-centered houses are common in the small villages in the country's northern and central regions. In the south, houses are built from *pise*, a mixture of straw and river mud. In the mountain areas, entire villages may be built of local stone.

pise
pees-AY

Housing Styles

In both the city and the country, traditional Moroccan houses have a similar style. The outside looks like whitewashed squares. Windows are small and covered by wrought-iron grills. Moroccans consider their homes quite private, and it's not easy to see from the outside in or from the inside out.

The centerpiece of many Moroccan homes is a private, open-air courtyard. Wealthy Moroccans often have a fountain in their courtyards. Fountains are a symbol of wealth in a desert country. The family courtyard serves as the gathering space for the whole family. The floor is usually concrete or dirt, but in wealthy homes it can be made of mosaic tile. Rural families often decorate their courtyards with fresh herbs or flowers. The family's living quarters—including kitchen and bedrooms—surround the courtyard. Urban families may live in apartments without courtyards.

As teens grow older, friendships outside the home become more and more important.

3 Friends & Family

TEENS IN MOROCCO DON'T THINK OF THEMSELVES AS AFRICAN, ARAB, BERBER, OR EUROPEAN, ALTHOUGH THEIR CULTURE BORROWS FROM ALL THESE CULTURES.

Moroccans are uniquely Moroccan. Walking through a Moroccan city, you'd find it hard to guess which country you are in, or even which continent. You might see groups of teens and young adults dressed in European clothes, sipping coffee at a sidewalk café. You'll certainly see street signs written in French. You might also notice women wearing headscarves and long robes, and men in traditional Muslim robes. Next to the French street signs, you'll see the distinctive script of the Arabic language. Throughout the crowd, you'll see skin colors ranging from the dark brown of sub-Saharan Africans to the pale white of Europeans.

Morocco is in Africa, but Moroccans are a mix of Arabs, indigenous Berber (or Amazigh) tribes, European colonists, and sub-Saharan African immigrants. This combination has led to a unique people that share diverse cultures, practice one religion (Islam), and place a high value on family.

Children's Names

Today almost all young Moroccans have Arabic names except in areas where Amazigh language and culture are still predominant. There, Amazigh names are more common. Some names overlap both cultures. The most popular overlaps are Mohamed, Fatima, and Aicha.

Common Amazigh Girls' Names in Morocco

Fadma
Ijja
Itto
Izza
Khadduj

Common Amazigh Boys' Names in Morocco

Brahim
Hamid
Hammou
Lehsen
Moha

Common Arabic Girls' Names in Morocco

Aicha
Fatima
Habiba
Hanan
Jamilah
Nabila
Salima
Zahra

Common Arabic Boys' Names in Morocco

Ahmad
Ali
Driss
Habib
Hakeem
Jamal
Khalil
Muhammad
Omar

A Diverse People

Most Moroccans have dark hair and olive skin, but their ethnic roots are so varied that it's not uncommon to see blond or black hair, pale skin, black skin, or brown and blue eyes in one group of friends.

The original inhabitants of Morocco were Berber, or, as they prefer to be called, Amazigh, which means "free man" in their language. They have lived in North Africa for thousands of years. Scientists are not sure where the Amazigh people came from before they lived in Morocco, Algeria, and Tunisia. The Amazigh

Camels are an important resource to Morocco's seminomadic Amazigh people.

were never homogenous; instead they were a collection of tribes with similar ethnicities and cultures and lived across a wide area. Every Amazigh tribe had its own languages and customs.

While the Amazigh people are Morocco's largest ethnic group—an estimated 60 percent of Moroccans fall into this category—almost all Moroccan Amazigh families have mixed at some point with Arabs, who moved to Morocco about 1,200 years ago. The Arabs brought their religion, Islam, and their language, Arabic. Amazigh and Arabs intermarried for centuries, and most began practicing Islam. Many also began speaking Arabic. Arabs tended to settle in Morocco's larger cities. They built most of the buildings that still exist in the older parts of Casablanca, Agadir, Rabat, and Fes.

Physically, the two peoples look similar, and it's almost impossible to tell an Amazigh from an Arab by appearance. Moroccans who live in cities today tend to be more Arab and to speak Arabic, while the few areas where

Amazigh Discrimination?

Many Moroccan Amazigh are feeling increasingly discriminated against in their own country. Although nearly 60 percent of Moroccans have Amazigh roots, the culture, and especially the language, is becoming rare. All school classes are taught in Arabic—even those in predominantly Amazigh areas. In 2004, some classes were offered in Amazigh, and there is an effort to make the language a required subject in all Moroccan schools. But while children in Amazigh areas—mostly in the mountain regions of Morocco—learn to read and write in Arabic, and perhaps Amazigh, their parents often can't read and write at all and speak only Amazigh. Further, all official business in Morocco must be conducted in Arabic, even in Amazigh areas.

The practice of henna, or temporary body art, has been a part of Moroccan culture since the Amazigh people first migrated to the area.

Amazigh is the primary language are in the country's poorer mountain areas. In the late 1990s, between 35 percent and 40 percent of Moroccans were estimated to live in mainly Amazigh areas and to speak an Amazigh dialect. With the trend of rural Moroccans' deciding to move to the cities in search of jobs and a more modern lifestyle, that percentage is falling rapidly.

Tangier is the last stop for those seeking a new life in Europe. It has been projected that there are more than 2.5 million Moroccan immigrants worldwide.

Many Moroccans also have European ties. Morocco is the African country that lies closest to the European continent. The port city of Tangier, along Morocco's northern Mediterranean Sea coast, is only nine miles (14.4 kilometers) from Spain, over the Strait of Gibraltar. Spain has a long history of conquering, being conquered by, supporting, and fighting with Morocco. Today many northern Moroccans continue to speak Spanish. France, though, has had a larger influence on Morocco. Morocco has a long history with France.

Today it is still common to see and hear the French language in Moroccan cities.

Finally, today's Moroccans have been influenced by their African neighbors to the south. The vast Sahara desert has always made travel between northern and southern Africa difficult, so the two regions are quite distinct. However, at times in Moroccan history, slaves were imported from sub-Saharan Africa. Their descendants continue to live in Morocco. More recently, other Africans have migrated north to Morocco to escape the violence and intense poverty of many sub-Saharan countries, and some even try to cross to Europe.

Devoted to Islam

A group of teens has gathered on one of Rabat's city squares after school. The teens laugh and joke with each other, discussing plans for the coming weekend. They stop joking when they hear a chanted call to prayer coming from the pointed top of a nearby minaret, or mosque tower.

While Moroccans are quite diverse ethnically, almost all practice one religion. Nearly 99 percent of Moroccans are Muslim, and the customs and culture of Islam are woven into all aspects of Moroccan life. Islam is an ancient religion practiced by more than 1 billion people worldwide. The heart of Islam is the belief that there is one Almighty God, Allah. The Muslim holy book, the Qur'an, describes in detail how Muslims should dedicate their lives

Religious Freedom

Although nearly all Moroccans practice Islam, the country's constitution states that Moroccans are free to practice other religions as well. This is unusual for predominantly Muslim countries, where national law often enforces Islamic culture and forbids many non-Islamic practices. In Morocco, while many Islamic practices are followed by many people—such as wearing a head-covering scarf by women—everybody is free to choose which customs they will follow and which they won't. People make those decisions based on their own feelings as well as the habits of their families. Even though they are a tiny minority, a small number of Moroccan Jews and Christians enjoy religious freedom and full civil rights.

to serving Allah. Muslims call Christians and Jews "people of the Book," because all three religions share many parts of the Bible's Old Testament, as well as the belief in only one god.

Five pillars, or requirements, guide Muslims in their daily activities. The first is to believe that Allah is God and Muhammad is his prophet. A second is to pray five times a day.

Although Europe is a short distance away, the Arab influence remains a strong part of Moroccan life. Moroccans have been practicing Islam since the Arabs introduced it in 670.

FRIENDS & FAMILY

Minarets

Tall, thin towers called minarets are distinctive parts of Islamic mosques. Unlike the round or tapered minarets found in other countries, Moroccan minarets are usually square, and the older ones are often decorated with green or blue tiles. The world's tallest minaret is at the Hassan II mosque in Casablanca, which stands at 693 feet (210 meters). The mosque is the second-largest religious site in the world (after Mecca), and it can hold 25,000 worshippers inside, with another 80,000 outside. It also has a retractable roof. Religious men called *muezzin* use the minarets to call Muslims to prayer. Muezzins have been calling faithful Muslims to prayer in this same manner for centuries, although today they are often aided by a loudspeaker.

muezzin
mu-WEDD-in

Built to withstand earthquakes, the Hassan II mosque has a heated floor, electric doors, a sliding roof, and a laser that can be seen 22 miles (35 km) away. It uses Islamic architecture, with traditional tile mosaics, carved plaster, and painted wood ceilings.

The last three are to observe the fast of Ramadan, to give money to help the poor, and if they can afford it, to make at least one journey to the Muslim holy city of Mecca, in Saudi Arabia.

Family Ties

If you ask Moroccans of any age what is most important to them, they will most likely reply "my family." Moroccan teens have friends whom they go to

The new family code in Morocco allows the children of non-Moroccan fathers to receive Moroccan citizenship. In the past, they were not allowed to become citizens, making it difficult to obtain official documents like passports or visas.

school with, play sports with, and hang out with. Many friends are likely to be cousins, and they spend much of their free time with their siblings, parents, aunts, uncles, and grandparents. On a weekend morning, a Moroccan teen is most likely to be home with his or her family.

The family has always been the cornerstone of life in Morocco, but the size, shape, and responsibilities of the family have changed over the past few decades. Until the first half of the 20th century, having more than one wife—a practice called polygamy that is legal in Islamic societies—was common for the few men who could afford it. However, this practice is almost nonexistent today. This, and the fact that more women are working outside the home and marrying much later, have reduced the average number of children born per woman by 50 percent in the last 30 years.

Traditional marriages were arranged like a business deal between two families, usually without the bride and the groom even meeting in advance. Once a couple was married, the husband was expected to provide housing and food for his wife, but he—and the rest of his family—controlled most of the wife's activities. According to Islamic custom, women usually remained at home and talked mostly with other women in their family and neighborhood.

Today few marriages are arranged, except in some of Morocco's most

remote areas. Many young people meet on their own first, and nearly all will ask their parents' consent to marry. Modern Moroccan men marry only one wife and have only two or three children. The importance of the family remains strong, and most Moroccan teens have close relationships with their grandparents, uncles, aunts, and cousins.

In 2004, the government established a "family code," also known as the Mudawana. This code declares that husbands and wives are equally responsible for caring for the family, and women no longer have to submit to the male of the family. The minimum marrying age was set at 18 for both sexes (previously the minimum age for girls was 15).

In the past, men could orally divorce their wives at any time, and the decision would be legal. Now, according to the new code, the couple must go to a judge who tries to reconcile them before approving a divorce. Women were also allowed to keep custody of their children and to be their own guardians. This is important, because it gives women a choice in their fate.

Another step taken to help divorcing women was described by Layla Rhiwi, a legal adviser in Morocco:

Under the new family code, whoever keeps the children keeps the marital house. So they [divorced wives] will no longer be on the streets. This is an important protection for women.

49

Hundreds of thousands of sheep are slaughtered during the Moroccan feast Aid-El-Kebir, which is also known as the "Feast of Sacrifice."

4

Festivals & Celebrations

IT'S EARLY MORNING IN CASABLANCA, AND TWO BROTHERS ARE HARD AT WORK IN THEIR FAMILY'S COURTYARD. The boys climb onto the flat roof of their house and return with a lamb. In crowded Moroccan cities, many families raise lambs on the roofs, and this family has been "fattening up" this lamb for a month. After their father returns from religious services at the mosque, he will slaughter it for a feast. It's Aid-El-Kebir, one of Morocco's most important feast days. This holiday celebrates a famous story from the Qur'an (as well as the Torah and the Bible):

Abraham's willingness to sacrifice his son for his God. Moroccans mark the day by slaughtering a lamb and preparing a feast. The family gathers to eat and then gives leftover meat to others who can't afford a whole lamb on this special day. Families spend the rest of the day visiting with friends and relatives.

Moroccans love to celebrate special days with gatherings involving large meals and family. In Morocco, because of the large population that practices Islam, Muslim holidays are also national holidays. Most Muslim holidays follow customs that have been around for centuries. Some of these, like Aid-El-Kebir, are celebrated across Morocco. Other Moroccan holidays are relatively new: Several state holidays have been established since the country gained its independence in 1956.

Fasting and Feasting

It is early evening in a small town along Morocco's Atlantic coast, and people seem to be hurrying somewhere. Most of the stores are closed. The town's few sidewalk cafes and coffee shops are empty. Men, women, and children walk briskly toward their homes. It's the Muslim holy month of Ramadan, and people are preparing to break their fast.

Since before the sun rose in the morning, Muslims have had nothing to eat or drink. Now, as the sun is beginning to set, they will have a small celebration with their families. Many families enjoy a rich bowl of tomato-based soup, followed by sweet pastries. In the morning, family members will wake up

Islamic Calendar

Muslim holidays are linked to the Islamic calendar, which is based on 12 lunar months. Each new month begins with the new moon. The first 11 months alternate in length between 29 days and 30 days; the 11th month has 30 days for 11 years in a row, followed by one year of 29 days. This pattern keeps the Islamic calendar in step with the phases of the moon and makes it about 11 days shorter than the Western calendar each year.

This means that Muslim holidays fall in different months of the Western calendar over the years. Moroccans use the Islamic calendar for religious holidays, not the Western, or Gregorian, calendar. For example, in 2005, the first day of Ramadan, which begins during the ninth month of the Islamic calendar, was October 2. In 2006, the holiday fell on September 23, and in 2007 on September 12.

early so they can have breakfast before the sun comes up. Once the sun is up, they will have nothing to eat and drink again until the sun is down. Muslims around the world celebrate Ramadan by praying and fasting. The month marks the time when, Muslims believe, the angel Gabriel's messages from Allah,

Markets are especially busy during Ramadan, when dates and other dried fruits are popular foods during the fasting month.

Public Holidays

These holidays commemorate significant days in Moroccan history

New Year's Day	January 1
Independence Manifesto	January 11
Labor Day	May 1
National Day	May 23
Feast of the Throne	July 30
Allegiance of Wadi-Eddahab	August 14
Day of the King and People's Revolution	August 20
Young People's Day	August 21
Anniversary of the Green March	November 6
Independence Day	November 18

the Muslim name for God, were passed to the Prophet Muhammad. They were later written in the holy book called the Qur'an. Observing this time of self-denial by fasting and praying is one of the five pillars of Islam. There is an air of celebration after breaking the fast at sunset. Teens often go out with family or friends and stroll for hours, shopping and greeting people they know.

After 28 days of Ramadan, Moroccans begin peering into the night sky. Once they see the crescent shape of the new moon, they know they will hear the official word from their mosque that Ramadan has ended. Then they begin the celebration of Eid al-Fitr. While much work and business activity slowed or paused during Ramadan, Eid al-Fitr brings the country to a halt for two or three days. Special meals have been prepared, homes have been cleaned, and new clothes have been purchased. The entire country celebrates the end of the fasting month.

Families and friends gather for meals and to relax together, and a mood of joyfulness settles around the country. In keeping with another of the five pillars of Islam, families donate to the poor during this time of celebration.

Another two-day feasting holiday is Eid Mawlid. This marks the birthday of the prophet Muhammad. It begins on either the 12th or the 17th day of the third month of the Islamic calendar. For two days, feasts and parades are held throughout the country, and individual families gather for large meals. At these gatherings, young children often recite poems about Muhammad.

Another celebrated Muslim holiday in Morocco is Achoura, a 10-day festival beginning on the first day of Fatih Mouharam, the first month of the Islamic calendar and Islamic New Year. Achoura includes games, banquets, and

Day of the King and the People's Revolution

On August 20 each year, Morocco marks the day in 1953 when France—then the colonial ruler of Morocco—forced King Mohammed V and the rest of the Moroccan royal family to leave their country. The French forced this exile because the king would not officially speak out against the large public protests against French rule in Morocco. France hoped to end these protests by this show of power, but instead the Moroccan public became more outraged by the forced exile of their king. Violent displays took place across the country, and today people see the exile as the beginning of the end of French rule. Protests and fighting continued for just over two years, until November 16, 1955. On this day, King Mohammed V returned triumphantly to his homeland. The following year, he negotiated for Morocco's freedom, and the country officially declared independence from France on March 2, 1956.

music. On the last day of Achoura, families fast together in memory of Muhammad, who fasted on this day in thanks to God for saving the prophet Moses.

Allegiance of Wadi-Eddahab

This public holiday on August 14 each year recognizes the date in 1974 when Morocco officially took control of the Wadi-Eddahab area of the Western Sahara. While Morocco claims political control of this area, the United Nations and most countries do not recognize its claim. A group called the Polisario Front Independence Movement, along with the Sahrawi Arab Democratic Republic, which claims to be the Western Sahara's legitimate government, has been trying to regain control of the area since 1976. Who controls it has yet to be resolved.

Local Celebrations

Across the open desert, a dozen riders on horseback come galloping into view. Soon the air fills with the sounds of their rifles firing as the horses charge at full speed. The horses are adorned with brightly colored and embroidered saddles. The riders are wearing traditional loose robes, and their heads are

Nearly 1,000 troops and 15,000 horses participate in fantasia demonstrations.

wrapped in turbans. They seem to be rushing directly at a group of people, but the people appear anything but frightened. They cheer on the riders, who come to a sudden, complete stop just as they reach the spectators. Then, swirling in the dust, the riders are off to repeat their charge.

This dramatic display, called a *fantasia*, is the high point of many local festivals across Morocco. These festivals, or *moussems*, are important throughout the year in all parts of Morocco— in small towns, large cities,

fantasia
fahn-ta-SEE-ah
moussems
MOO-sems

and even the most remote desert areas. Moussems honor local holy men. They take place wherever the holy man's tomb is. These tombs, called *kooubba*, are usually white, dome-shaped buildings that may be in the middle of a vast desert, on a rocky mountain slope, or in the middle of a crowded city. Some moussems, like the one honoring Moulay Idriss, the founder of Morocco's first major Muslim empire around 780, are huge events—Morocco's king regularly attends. Other festivals are much smaller. They usually serve as annual gatherings for whatever region they take place in. Moussems often take place after the harvest, when people have extra cash and free time.

kooubba
KOO-bah

In larger cities, moussems are a unique celebration and may resemble other major Islamic feast days. Families often wear new clothes, take the day off from school or work, pray, eat, and visit with each other. In the country, moussems are once-a-year opportunities for people who don't see each other the rest of the year. Rural teens may dress up in traditional clothes and jewelry that has been passed down from generation to generation. They may walk, ride donkeys or mules, or, if they own one, ride in the family's truck to get to the moussem. Often marriages are arranged at moussems, and teens as young as 14 sometimes meet their future spouses at these events. No matter what the circumstances are, Muslims never forget that honoring a holy person is the reason for the celebration. Between the socializing, feasting, and dancing, there is always prayer in which Muslims thank Allah for blessings they have received or ask him for a favor.

National Holidays

Other holidays mark the nation's history as an independent state. Although Morocco's rich history stretches back thousands of years, the nation has only been an independent country since 1956. State, or public, holidays, unlike religious holidays, are based on the Western calendar.

Independence Day falls on November 18. The holiday marks the day that Morocco became independent of France's control. Green March Remembrance Day, on November 6, commemorates the day that more than 350,000 Moroccan civilians, or nonmilitary residents, marched into the Western Sahara in 1975 to emphasize Morocco's claim to power over that region.

Perhaps the most important state holiday of the year is the Festival of the Throne, or Throne Day. This annual holiday, on July 30, marks the day that King Mohammed VI succeeded his father, King Hassan II, on Morocco's throne in 1999. Since his ascension to power, Mohammed has made a considerable

King Mohammed VI uses Throne Day to assess the state of the country, as well as to outline his plans for the coming year.

effort to modernize the country and improve Morocco's standard of living.

Teens and young children take part in parades, watch spectacular fireworks, and celebrate with music, food, and dancing. The royal palace also hosts a large reception, and the king makes a speech to the nation. Like some of Morocco's other major holidays, Throne Day has celebrations that sometimes last for several days.

Olive farms are expected to double in acreage by 2010, to more than 2.5 million acres (1 million hectares).

5 Finding a Place to Work

FOR TEENS AS WELL AS ADULTS, JOBS ARE HARD TO FIND IN MOROCCO.

The national unemployment rate—the number of people looking for work who can't find a job—is 7.7 percent. In urban areas, the rate is around 20 percent. That means one in five working-age, urban Moroccans is unemployed. Another 20 percent of people of working age have left the country to seek employment abroad.

The job outlook is even more grim for recent high school graduates; it's estimated that about one-third of them are without jobs. Even among Morocco's top students—the fewer than 300,000 who attend a university—about 11 percent cannot get a job after graduation.

It's not that Morocco has a poor economy—the country has thriving agricultural, mining, manufacturing, and tourism industries. The large number of young people means that more and more jobs need to be created each year just to keep everyone employed. Although Morocco has booming industries, its population is growing faster than its economy.

Working Students

A tour guide speaks to five British tourists at the entrance to the tomb of Mohammed V. "When Morocco gained its independence in 1956, Sultan Mohammed Ben Youssef changed his title to King Mohammed V, which he felt sounded more modern," explains the tour guide, who is also a student at the Mohammed V University in Rabat.

The guide studies economics and political science and hopes to find a job with the government. In the meantime, she earns money as many of her fellow students do: providing tours in French and English to the thousands of international visitors who come to Morocco's capital city each year. She attends classes for about six hours a day, then heads to the tomb of Mohammed V, where she seeks out tourists who want to hear more about the tomb in English or French—two languages she has learned to speak fluently at school. Back at her university dormitory in the evening, she settles in for four or five hours of homework.

Many students work as tour

Working in France

Since almost all Moroccans speak some French, France is a natural destination for those who leave the country to look for work. For several decades, Moroccans have moved to France for that reason. They have been able to adapt to the culture relatively easily—they already speak the language and are familiar with many French customs left behind by their former colonizers. However, in recent years, Moroccans living and working in France have encountered prejudice and resentment. One reason is that jobs in France—which were plentiful 20 years ago—have become harder to find. Some people feel that Moroccans and other immigrants are taking jobs away from French people. Another reason is that Europeans and other Westerners have grown increasingly intolerant of Muslims.

guides because of their language skills. Although most people speak some French, only younger, more educated Moroccans speak the language well enough—and without an Arabic accent—to be paid for their services. More and more high school and university students are also learning English, which

Unemployed university students have staged several demonstrations demanding their right to employment.

is another language commonly used by tourists. Some students also learn German and Spanish, which are both popular in northern Morocco. Besides language skills, Moroccan students also have a good knowledge of their country's history and are able to provide factual details that tourists want to hear.

Explaining Moroccan history to tourists is not a career goal for most Moroccan university students. They view it as an enjoyable job to support themselves while they are in school. They usually provide services "unofficially," meaning they do not report their earnings or pay taxes. But upon graduation, many young educated Moroccans find that they cannot find a job in the industry they trained for. Many university graduates, regardless of their degree, continue to work in tourism, or they leave Morocco in search of better job opportunities elsewhere.

Farming: National Occupation

Miles south of the capital city of Rabat, another young Moroccan is also at work. This rural Moroccan left school at age 14 to help support her family. She spends her days in a lush orange grove picking fruit to be shipped across Morocco as well as outside of the country. Orange growing is a big business in Morocco; other important crops are lemons, tangerines, and olives. It may seem surprising that such crops are grown in a country on the edge of the Sahara desert, but Morocco has a very Mediterranean climate. The temperature during the country's hottest months only averages 75 to 85 degrees Fahrenheit (24 to 29 degrees Celsius). Morocco has a vast system of irrigation—pipes laid along the ground to move water—to

Working Women

In 2006, about 27 percent of all workers in Morocco were women. Many of these women work in agriculture and service jobs, but some also work in professional jobs. One-third of doctors and one-quarter of university professors in Morocco are women. One study estimates that more than 100,000 women from rural areas are employed in urban areas as household workers. Gender equality is an important issue. In 2002, King Mohammed VI reserved 30 of the 325 Chamber of Representatives seats for women. By 2002, women held 34 seats, making Morocco the only Arab nation to have women making up 10 percent of the parliament. Rwanda has the greatest number of women in parliament in both Africa and the world, at nearly 50 percent. Egypt has the lowest number in Africa, at around 2 percent.

Tourism as a Growing Industry

Tourism is a booming business in Morocco. Europeans and others come to experience the country's unique culture, the ancient architecture of the mosques and medinas in the major cities, and the beautiful sun and sand along the Mediterranean and Atlantic coasts. With just a short plane ride from Europe, tourists can choose among the exotic culture of Morocco's ancient cities, adventurous treks through remote mountains or deserts, and luxurious accommodations at world-class hotels and beach resorts.

Around 6.5 million tourists visit Morocco every year. The government hopes to increase the numbers to 10 million tourists by 2010.

Morocco's national drink is mint tea, and the country is one of the biggest importers of tea in the world.

foster crop growing.

Nearly 40 percent of Morocco's labor force works in agriculture. Almost all of these farmers work on small family farms, but the combined crop output is enough to make Morocco a major exporter of fruits and vegetables to Europe. With its warm, southern climate, Moroccan-grown crops ripen a few weeks earlier than most European crops. This gives Morocco an edge in the European market.

Morocco
Population density
and political map

SPAIN

Ceuta
(SPAIN)

Mediterranean
Sea

Tangier

Tétouan

Melilla
(SPAIN)

Oujda

Kenitra

Fès

Rabat

Meknès

Casablanca

Safi

N
W   E
S

Marrakech

ATLANTIC
OCEAN

Agadir

ALGERIA

Laâyoune

SAQUIA EL HAMRA

0   100   200 mi.
0   100   200 km

Semara

Boujdour

Western Sahara
(administered by
MOROCCO)

Dakhla

WADI-EDDAHAB

MAURITANIA

Population Density
(People per square km)

More than 200

24–200

5–24

1–4

Irrigation pools collect groundwater during the day. In the evening, they are drained to water crops, to use for cleaning, and to serve as a water supply for livestock.

Even with the irrigation systems, water shortages often cause major trouble for Moroccan farmers. In drought years—when rainfall is scarce—many farmers can lose their entire crop. This makes it hard for farmers to earn a steady living, and most of Morocco's farmers earn low incomes. While the legal minimum wage in all other industries is about 1,842 dirhams (U.S. $235) a month, in agriculture it is only 1,183 dirhams (U.S. $151) per month. Morocco's government is working to extend irrigation to more of the country. Although recent droughts have

Division of Labor

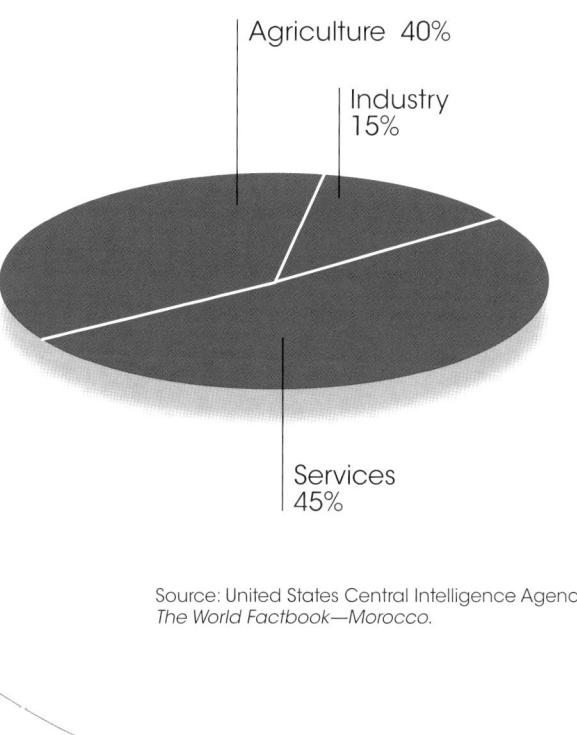

Agriculture 40%

Industry
15%

Services
45%

Source: United States Central Intelligence Agency.
The World Factbook—Morocco.

made water conservation and distribution difficult, the government is using several types of irrigation in an attempt to find out which one works best with the country's climate.

This would help protect more farmers in times of drought and, in turn, would strengthen Morocco's entire agricultural economy.

Phosphates: National Treasure

Teens in many parts of the world have never heard of the mineral phosphate, but in Morocco almost everyone is aware of this valuable resource. Phosphates are mined from the earth and made into fertilizer used by farmers across the world. Morocco has about two-thirds of the world's available phosphates, and phosphate-related products are the country's top export.

In several cities in western Morocco, the tall smokestacks of phosphate processing plants poke high into the sky. Phosphate factories are a symbol of Morocco's modern manufacturing industry. They are also a symbol of the country's new environmental problems. Processing phosphates requires many chemicals and produces smoke that hurts the environment. Moroccans who live near phosphate plants are used to a thin haze of dust in the air and an unsafe chemical in their water. Because of this, most drink bottled water if they can afford it. Figuring out how to increase phosphate mining production and make it safer for the environment is

Damaging the Environment?

Phosphate production lowers the quality of Morocco's air and water, but it's not the country's only environmental hazard. Many aspects of Morocco's modernizing economy also damage the land and water. For centuries, Moroccans farmed only what they needed to feed themselves and did not harm the earth in the process. Today's huge food-export industry does more damage. For instance, Morocco exports olives and related products such as olive oil around the world. This brings money into the country, but it has an oily side effect: margines, the remnants of the squeezed olives and other by-products created during oil processing. Margines can be dried and used as fuel, but they are more often disposed of in rivers and lakes. The margines create a slick film on the water's surface and absorb the water's oxygen, destroying the ecosystem. Processing olives in factories also pollutes the air.

Morocco is well-known for its leatherwork and its old-fashioned tanneries. However, the manufacturing of leather produces numerous by-products that are released into the air and water.

important for Morocco's future. Many of today's top students will work on this problem as engineers and scientists.

Processing phosphate is one of Morocco's most important manufacturing activities, but it's not the only one.

Many Moroccans work in factories that produce clothing, leather, shoes, car and truck parts, and household appliances. Young adults with technical training find work in factories that produce electronic devices like computers, electronic games, and television sets. The large supply of these kinds of skilled workers means that this type of manufacturing is increasing in Morocco.

Beaches are popular hangouts for teens. Around 90 percent of Morocco's beaches have been deemed safe for swimming—the remaining 10 percent are too polluted or are otherwise contaminated.

6

Life & Leisure

IT'S A LATE SUMMER AFTER-NOON IN THE CITY OF MARRAKECH, AND THE MEDINA IS JUST COMING TO LIFE. Shopkeepers are removing their wooden shutters, signaling the end of the afternoon rest period. Stores have been closed and people have stayed inside their cooler homes. Now the medina's lanes are filling with shoppers. Women with small children stroll by, buying small items like toys and clothing.

Just outside the medina, a group of teens gathers at the edge of a jam-packed square. Pop music blares from a small battery-operated radio, and friends laugh and joke with each other. Brilliantly colored tents, stalls, and carts fill the area. Acrobats perform complex tricks. Pipe players add their own tunes to the clamor, and water sellers ring noisy brass bells as they offer their goods to the crowd. This is Djemaa el Fna, Marrakech's famous open-air entertainment square, where performers and residents have come each evening at dusk for centuries. Each space in the square showcases a talent. Snake charmers, musicians, storytellers, and acrobats are mainstays of the nightly performances.

Arts & Crafts

Moroccan arts and crafts are recognized throughout the world. The capital city of Rabat is famous for hand-knotted carpets. These carpets borrow a Turkish design of intricate borders surrounding a central geometric symbol. In much of the rest of the country, Amazigh tribes weave rugs with geometric patterns passed down from one generation to the next. Metalwork shops, where craftsmen gently hammer brass and silver into elaborate teapots, trays, and small boxes, can be found in almost any medina. Metal is also worked into bracelets, necklaces, rings, and earrings—with designs varying by region. Potters in the cities of Fes, Marrakech, Safi, and Meknes are internationally known for their bold, colorful bowls and serving platters.

The colors, patterns, motifs, and techniques used to make rugs vary by region.

Djemaa el Fna is unique to Marrakech, but the ambience of the nightly gathering reflects the national attitude toward leisure time. It incorporates the country's traditions in a simple way for people to enjoy at their own pace. Moroccans believe in taking the time to enjoy the richness of their culture. They tend to appreciate gathering and relaxing—usually with good food, music, and other entertainment. Nevertheless, the country's varied geography of coastline, desert, and mountains offers ample opportunity for sports such as golf, soccer, and mountain trekking. The country's cultural influences have helped to popularize a variety of art and musical forms.

As the country becomes more connected, the Internet becomes more important. Even the more remote areas of Morocco have cyber cafes. Although using the Web is an expensive hobby that usually costs between 5 and 10 dirhams (U.S. 64 cents–$1.27) an hour, millions of Moroccans access the Internet on a regular basis.

Moroccan teens frequent the 1,500 to 3,000 cyber cafes across the country to surf the Internet, catch the latest news, and meet new friends.

Low-Key Leisure

Like all aspects of Moroccan life, family is the center of most leisure activities.

Teens spend most of their free time with family members, and a lot of a family's relaxing is done around the home. Income makes a big difference in how families spend their free time. Families without electricity, whether in a crowded city neighborhood or a remote rural area, tend to gather in the evenings around a battery-operated radio or TV.

Those with electricity may watch one of the two government-run television stations, which broadcast mostly in Arabic and sometimes in French. Only about five to 10 minutes of news is reported in an Amazigh language.

For the many families with a satellite dish, international channels like CNN, Al Jazeera, and Dubai TV may be on the screen. VCRs are common, and there is an active market for foreign DVDs. Action films are popular among teens, because the language used in them is not too important.

The ways that families spend time together around the home are influenced by how traditional they are. In traditional culture, women and men remain separated for most of the day. While men go out of the home and socialize with other men, women mostly stay at home and socialize with other women. Today some traditional families still observe these customs, but in others, all the members of a family relax together.

Moroccan teens don't spend all their leisure time with their families. Teens in bigger cities join their friends at soda bars and public parks. Landscaped gathering spots are one of the contributions made by the French. The parks are usually filled with groups of young people, families with young children, and couples. Students often find a quiet spot in a park for studying or relaxing. Taking long walks that end with a rest in a park is a daily habit for many.

Just as with inside activities, Moroccan men and women often have separate destinations when they go out. Many men spend most of their day with other men. After work they may gather at a coffee shop—where they are just

The news channel Al Jazeera has more than 40 million viewers in the Arab world. About one-fifth of these are Moroccan.

77

as likely to drink mint tea as coffee—to watch television or talk about sports or, on occasion, politics. More traditional Moroccan women head out only to shop for specific items or to take their children to a park. These women almost always wear a djellaba and a headscarf when they are in public. Younger people, including students and young couples, tend to go out for walks together and stop at sidewalk cafes or shop together.

Water Play

Much of Moroccan life is influenced by the country's relative lack of water. So Moroccans are used to making the most of available water. Every city and larger town has a *hammam*, or public bath, and public swimming pools are quite common also.

For centuries, hammams have

hammam
HAA-mahm

Djellaba

Traditional Moroccan dress for both men and women is the *djellaba*, a loose-fitting, hooded robe with long sleeves. Some Moroccans continue to wear djellabas outside the home, while others wear them only on certain occasions. Some wear them only in public, with modern clothes underneath.

djellaba
jell-AH-buh

Both Western-style clothing and traditional djellabas are common wardrobe choices.

Although Morocco sees itself as belonging to a more liberal form of Islam, some religious leaders have spoken out against the Westernization of women.

served as bathing spots. Today they remain popular for regular bathing for families who don't have running water in their homes, as well as for those who just like to relax in the calming environment of a hammam. Women and men are separated—some facilities are single-sex, and some have different hours for women and for men. Tourists like to head to a hammam for a unique

Moroccan experience—all offer massages as well as bathing. Every urban Moroccan has probably been to a hammam, but they tend to be frequented more often by older generations, who meet their friends and socialize there.

Teens may gather at a local swimming pool. There are free pools in most of Morocco's cities, and they serve as gathering places for families, children, and groups of friends. At one point, the city of Casablanca was home to the Orthlieb pool, the world's longest swimming pool. The seawater pool was nearly 1,585 feet (483 m) long and nearly 250 feet (76 m) wide. The giant King Hassan II mosque now sits on the site of the former pool.

National Sport

A crowd gathers at the edge of an empty parking lot on the outskirts of Casablanca. Another crowd gathers outside an electronics shop on a busy shopping street in Rabat. On a sandy beach, young children and teens engage in a spontaneous competition. What's at the heart of all of these gatherings? Morocco's national sport: soccer.

Almost every schoolchild in Morocco knows the rules of soccer. Friends in the country, in small towns, or in large cities can usually find a spot for an impromptu game. When they're not playing soccer, they might be watching it on television. It's not uncommon

Attracting Tourists

With tourism becoming more and more important to Morocco's economy, the country is developing many activities to attract visitors. Along the coastal areas, water sports like scuba diving, windsurfing, and sailing are becoming more common. In many parts of the plains, golf courses have been built, and the Atlas Mountains now feature resorts for downhill and cross-country skiing. The parking lot at Morocco's largest downhill ski area is filled with 800 cars and buses every weekend. Mainly tourists and the wealthiest Moroccans enjoy these sports, but more and more average Moroccans are trying them out. Some public schools are beginning to sponsor clubs and trips to nearby ski areas.

Morocco's national soccer team, the Atlas Lions, was the first African nation to win a group competition at the World Cup.

جمعية كاتنا

to see crowds outside electronics stores or sidewalk cafes with televisions tuned to a soccer match.

Morocco has several professional soccer teams, and attending a match is a favorite outing for families, teens, and young couples. A Moroccan national team has appeared in World Cup matches four times. The country last hosted the African Cup of Nations in 1988. It's likely that, even as more sports and other leisure activities from various parts of the world gain popularity in Morocco, soccer will retain its status as the national sport.

Looking Ahead

MOROCCAN TEENS LIVE IN AN EVOLVING WORLD. Like their parents, they value the Muslim religious traditions shared by nearly everyone in their country. Also like their parents, they combine elements of the three major cultures—Arab, Amazigh, and French—that have shaped their young country. Most Moroccan teens speak at least two of those languages. Today's young people are much more likely than their parents were to go to school and to understand and use modern technology, such as computers and cell phones.

As Morocco struggles with increasingly high unemployment rates, many young people are moving to Europe in search of good jobs and a better future. Since they make up such a large share of their country's population, teens will have to work to ensure their culture's survival and strengthen their nation's economy.

At a Glance

Official name: Kingdom of Morocco

Capital: Rabat

People

Population: 33,757,175 (July 2007 est.)

Population by age group:
0–14 years: 31%
15–64 years: 63.9%
65 years and over: 5.1%

Life expectancy at birth: 71.2 years

Official language: Arabic

Other common languages: Amazigh dialects, French

Religion:
Muslim: 98.7%
Christian: 1.1%
Jewish: 0.2%

Legal ages:
Driver's license: 18
Marriage: 18
Military service: 18
Voting: 18

Government

Type of government: Constitutional monarchy

Chief of state: King

Head of government: Prime minister, appointed by monarch

Lawmaking body: Bicameral Parliament, with an upper house, or Chamber of Counselors, and a lower house, or Chamber of Representatives, elected

Administrative divisions: 15 regions (Morocco claims the territory of Western Sahara, the political status of which is considered undetermined by the U.S. government)

Independence: March 2, 1956 (from France)

National symbol: Solomon's Seal (green outlined five-pointed star depicted on national flag)

Geography

Total area: 178,620 square miles (446,550 sq km)

Climate: Mediterranean, but more extreme in the interior

Highest point: Jebel Toubkal, 13,745 feet (4,165 m)

Lowest point: Sebkha Tah, 182 feet (55 m) below sea level

Major rivers: Oued Moulouya, Oued Sebou, Oued Oum er Rbia

Major landforms: Atlas and Rif Mountains, Sahara Desert

Economy

Currency: Moroccan dirhams

Population below poverty line: 19%

Major natural resources: phosphates, iron ore, manganese, lead, zinc, fish, salt

Major agricultural products: barley, wheat, citrus fruits, wine, vegetables, olives, livestock

Major exports: clothing, fish, inorganic chemicals, crude minerals, fertilizers, petroleum products, fruits, vegetables

Major imports: crude petroleum, textiles, telecommunications equipment, wheat, natural gas, electricity, plastics

Historical Timeline

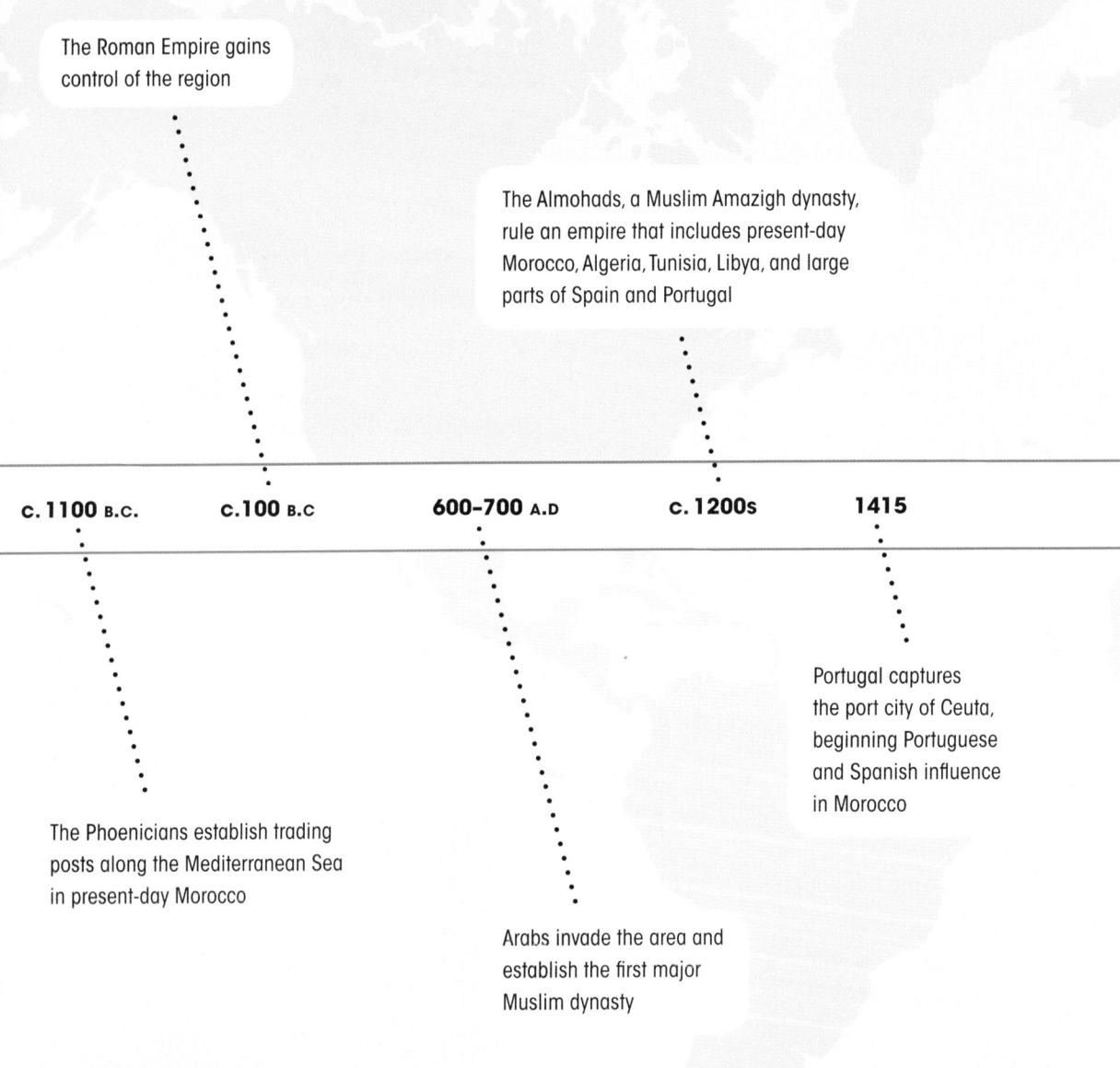

The Roman Empire gains control of the region

The Almohads, a Muslim Amazigh dynasty, rule an empire that includes present-day Morocco, Algeria, Tunisia, Libya, and large parts of Spain and Portugal

c. 1100 B.C.   **c.100** B.C   **600–700** A.D   **c. 1200s**   **1415**

Portugal captures the port city of Ceuta, beginning Portuguese and Spanish influence in Morocco

The Phoenicians establish trading posts along the Mediterranean Sea in present-day Morocco

Arabs invade the area and establish the first major Muslim dynasty

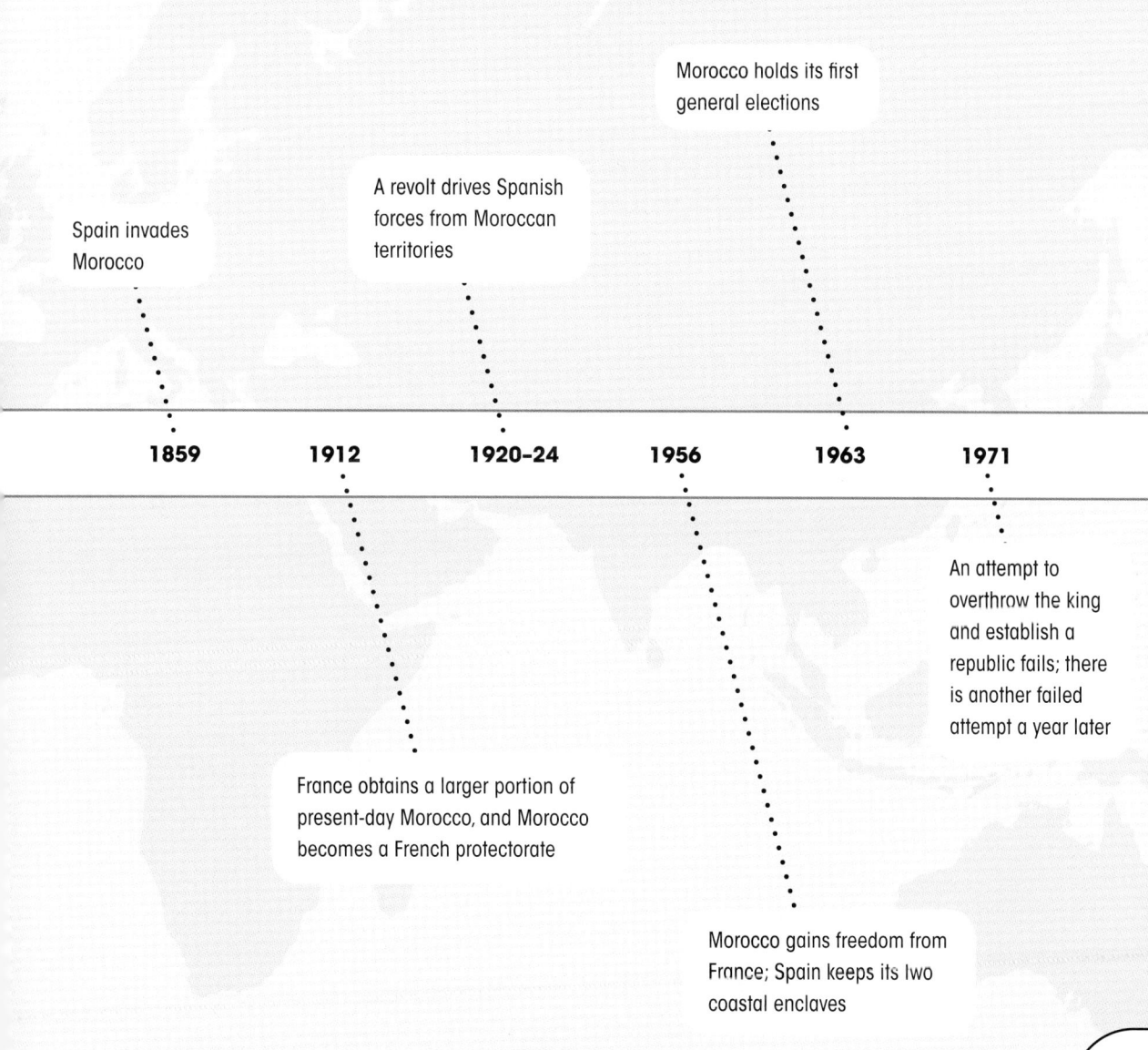

Spain invades
Morocco

A revolt drives Spanish
forces from Moroccan
territories

Morocco holds its first
general elections

1859 **1912** **1920–24** **1956** **1963** **1971**

France obtains a larger portion of
present-day Morocco, and Morocco
becomes a French protectorate

An attempt to
overthrow the king
and establish a
republic fails; there
is another failed
attempt a year later

Morocco gains freedom from
France; Spain keeps its two
coastal enclaves

87

Historical Timeline

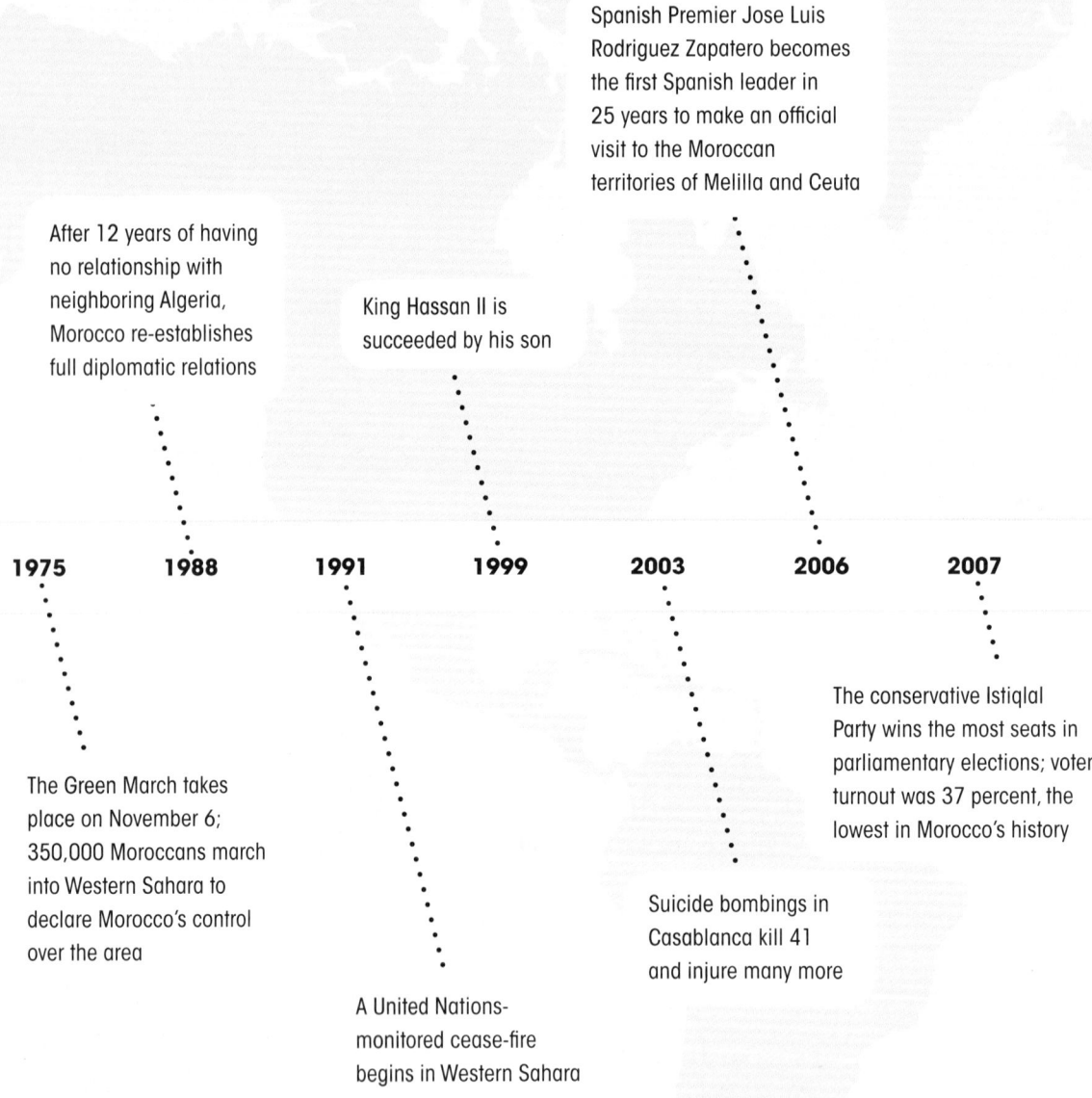

Spanish Premier Jose Luis Rodriguez Zapatero becomes the first Spanish leader in 25 years to make an official visit to the Moroccan territories of Melilla and Ceuta

After 12 years of having no relationship with neighboring Algeria, Morocco re-establishes full diplomatic relations

King Hassan II is succeeded by his son

1975   **1988**   **1991**   **1999**   **2003**   **2006**   **2007**

The conservative Istiqlal Party wins the most seats in parliamentary elections; voter turnout was 37 percent, the lowest in Morocco's history

The Green March takes place on November 6; 350,000 Moroccans march into Western Sahara to declare Morocco's control over the area

Suicide bombings in Casablanca kill 41 and injure many more

A United Nations-monitored cease-fire begins in Western Sahara

Glossary

diverse	varied or assorted
ethnicity	a person's national or cultural origins
homogeneous	similar throughout
indigenous	native to a place
inhabitants	people who live in a certain place
Islam	religion founded on the Arabian Peninsula in the seventh century by the prophet Muhammad
mosaic	a pattern or picture made of small pieces of colored stone, tile, or glass
mosque	the Islamic place of worship
protectorate	a country or region that is controlled and defended by a more powerful state
Qur'an	the holy book of Islam, which consists mainly of the revelations that Muslims believe Muhammad received from God during the seventh century
seminomad	a member of a tribe that wanders with livestock to graze part of the year
shantytown	informal settlements of low-cost dwellings

Additional Resources

IN THE LIBRARY

Fiction and nonfiction titles to further enhance your introduction to teens in Morocco, past and present.

Gaissa, Yasser. *Tales from Morocco.* Washington, D.C.: Amideast, 1995.

Lalami, Laila. *Hope and Other Dangerous Pursuits.* New York: Harvest Books, 2006.

Blauer, Ettagale. *Morocco: Enchantment of the World.* New York: Children's Press, 1999.

Delgado, Kevin. *Morocco.* San Diego: Lucent Books, 2005.

Di Piazza, Francesca Davis. *Morocco in Pictures.* Minneapolis: Lerner Publishing Group, 2006.

ON THE WEB

For more information on this topic, use FactHound.
1. Go to *www.facthound.com*
2. Type in this book ID: 075653402X
3. Click on the *Fetch It* button.

Look for more Global Connections books.

Teens in Australia	Teens in France	Teens in Mexico	Teens in Turkey
Teens in Brazil	Teens in Ghana	Teens in Nepal	Teens in the U.S.A.
Teens in Canada	Teens in India	Teens in Nigeria	Teens in Venezuela
Teens in China	Teens in Iran	Teens in Russia	Teens in Vietnam
Teens in Egypt	Teens in Israel	Teens in Saudi Arabia	
Teens in England	Teens in Japan	Teens in South Korea	
Teens in Finland	Teens in Kenya	Teens in Spain	

Source Notes

Page 21, caption: "Queen Rania Returns to Morocco." Rania Al-Abdullah, Queen of Jordan. Official Web site. 1 June 2007. 25 Sept. 2007. www.queenrania.jo/content/modulePopup.aspx?secID=&itemID=1553&ModuleID=press&ModuleOrigID=news

Page 22, column 1, line 9: Sarah Touahri. "Low Pass Rate for Baccalaureate Exams in Morocco." Magharebia: The News & Views of the Maghreb. 22 June 2007. 5 July 2007. www.magharebia.com/cocoon/awi/xhtml1/en_GB/features/awi/features/2007/06/22/feature-01

Page 28, column 2, line 8: Geoff D. Porter. "Tourism Meets Terrorism in Morocco." *The Daily Star*. 3 May 2007. 26 Sept. 2007. www.1stmediterranean.com/actuuk/archivesuk/resultat.php?id=1343

Page 32, column 2, line 5: "Morocco—Out-migration of rural youth." The International Fund for Agricultural Development. 15 July 2007. www.ifad.org/gender/learning/challenges/youth/m_6_3.htm

Page 34, column 2, line 26: Hassan M'Souli. *Morocco Modern*. Northhampton, Mass.: Interlink Books, 2005, p. 10.

Page 49, column 2, line 33: Pascale Harter. "Changing Status of Morocco's Shunned Wives." BBC News. 28 Jan. 2004. 23 July 2007. http://news.bbc.co.uk/2/hi/africa/3435153.stm

Pages 84-85, At a Glance: United States Central Intelligence Agency. *The World Factbook—Morocco*. 19 July 2007. 23 July 2007. www.cia.gov/library/publications/the-world-factbook/geos/mo.html

Select Bibliography

Agenor, Pierre Richard, and Karim El Aynaoui. "Labor Market Policies and Unemployment in Morocco." 7 Dec. 2007. 6 Oct. 2007. www1.worldbank.org/wbiep/macro-program/ agenor/pdfs/Immpa-Morocco.pdf

"Arts and Culture in Morocco." Morocco.com. 2007. 2 Oct. 2007. www.morocco.com/culture

BBC Timeline. "Morocco." BBC News. 11 Sept. 2007. 14 Oct. 2007. http://news.bbc.co.uk/1/hi/world/middle_east/country_profiles/2431365.stm

Bloom, Jonathan, and Blair, Sheila. *Islam: A Thousand Years of Faith and Power*. New Haven, Conn.: Yale University Press, 2002.

Clark, Nick. "Education in Morocco." World Education News & Reviews. April 2006. 3 August 2007. www.wes.org/ewenr/06apr/practical_morocco.htm

Davis, Susan S., and Douglas A. Davis. *Adolescence in a Moroccan Town: Making Social Sense*. New Brunswick, N.J.: Rutgers University Press, 1989.

Dillman, Bradford. "Morocco's Future: Arab, African, or European?" *Wafin: Moroccan Connections in America*. 11 Oct. 2007. 19 Oct. 2007. www.wafin.com/bradford.phtml

EarthTrends: The Environmental Information Portal. "Country Profile: Morocco." World Resources Institute. 2006. 15 Sept. 2007. http://earthtrends.wri.org/text/population-health/country-profile-126.html

Kasbah Itran. "Berber Culture." 23 August 2007. 1 Sept. 2007. www.kasbahitran.com/kasbah_en/03cultura/03cultura.html

Morocco Fact File. "Morocco." 2001. 15 Sept. 2007. www.iss.co.za/AF/profiles/Morocco/Morocco1.html#sec_info_Anchor

"Moroccan Government." Moroccan American Trade and Investment Council. 11 Oct. 2007. 17 Oct. 2007. www.moroccanamericantrade.com/morogov.cfm

Prengaman, Peter. "Morocco's Amazighs Battle to Keep From Losing Their Culture: Arab minority forces majority to abandon native language." *San Francisco Chronicle*. 16 March 2001. 15 Sept. 2007. www.sfgate.com/cgi-bin/article.cgi?file=/chronicle/archive/2001/03/16/MN145053.DTL%20

U.N. News Service. "Morocco: Western Sahara Dispute at Turning Point, Minister Tells U.N." AllAfrica.com. 1 Oct. 2007. 8 Oct. 2007. http://allafrica.com/stories/200710020015.html

U.S. Department of State. "Background Note: Morocco." 4 Oct. 2007. 15 Oct. 2007. www.state.gov/r/pa/ei/bgn/5431.htm

U.S. Social Security Administration. Social Security Programs Throughout the World: Africa, 2005." *Morocco*. www.ssa.gov/policy/docs/progdesc/ssptw/2004-2005/africa/morocco.html

Index

About the Author
Sandy Donovan

Sandy Donovan has written several books for young readers about history, economics, government, and other topics. She has also worked as a newspaper reporter, a magazine editor, and a Web site developer. She has a bachelor's degree in journalism and a master's degree in public policy, and lives in Minneapolis, Minnesota, with her husband and two sons.

About the Content Adviser
Susan Schaefer Davis, Ph.D.

Dr. Susan Schaefer Davis first went to Morocco with the Peace Corps in the 1960s. She has taught anthropology at Haverford College, Rutgers University, and Alakhawayn (Morocco) University, with work focusing on Moroccan adolescence and women; she has written a book on each. She also consults on socioeconomic development for agencies including the World Bank and USAID. The Web site *www.marrakeshexpress.org* shares her knowledge of Moroccan textiles, and allows readers to meet some young women weavers and learn about their lives.